Far More Satisfying Than Hell

AMY LAURENS

OTHER WORKS

Far More Satisfying Than Hell

INKLET #85

AMY LAURENS

Inkprint PRESS

www.inkprintpress.com

Print ISBN: 978-1-922434-25-8
eBook ISBN: 9798201932558

www.inkprintpress.com

National Library of Australia Cataloguing-in-Publication Data
Laurens, Amy 1985 –
Far More Satisfying Than Hell
42 p.
ISBN: 978-1-922434-25-8
Inkprint Press, Canberra, Australia
1. Fiction—Fantasy—Dark Fantasy 2. Fiction—Fantasy—Contemporary 2. Fiction—Short Stories

First Print Edition: July 2022
Cover photo © .shock via Deposit Photos
Cover design © Inkprint Press
Interior art © Amy Laurens

FAR MORE
SATISFYING THAN
HELL

IT WAS DARK, AND THERE WAS DARKness, and the two were not synonymous. Outside, Ava could hear the chirp of crickets, the slow bleep-blip of tiny frogs, and behind it all, the soprano piping of some other kind of insect, the whole orchestral riot punctuated every now and then by a splash from a fish or a duck in the pond, fulfilling the role of percussion.

Inside, in the sparse room of her prison, she could hear nothing.

Usually, if she listened very hard, Ava could find her own heartbeat in any stillness, a comforting metronome in the background of her days, marking out time until the end—the end of what she wasn't certain, but the end of something, for sure.

But it was dark, and there was darkness, and the darkness wasn't the dark that gleamed outside in the moonlight, nor the dim shadows in the corners of her room.

Instead, the darkness was a cloud, noxious and smothering and smelling vaguely of plastic, draping over her and weighing her down, dampening her other-worldly senses.

Her cheek twitched as her concentration slipped momentarily from frogs.

Fury boiled inside—but the darkness responded, contracting, clenching, tightening, and she forced her attention once more to the chorus of frogs and insects somewhere out there in the night, and the smell of pond water curling in through the barely-open window.

The pond was not that large, a hundred paces across perhaps on a good day, so 'somewhere out there' wasn't really a large area to contend with—unless of course you were a frog, knee-high to a towering blade of grass, that hundred-pace pond the entire summation of your world.

No wonder mortals had such limited perspective on things, living in a world that was barely bigger than a pond.

But that made her cheek twitch again, which made the darkness respond in kind, and so with a heavily exhalation, she closed her eyes cast her thoughts adrift till morning, concentrating on the taste of pondy water at the back of her throat, the smell of algae, and the singing chirpings of the frogs.

The darkness was easier to bear in daylight. Her captors had left her curtains flung wide open—for reasons unfathomable, since she was hardly going to turn to dust or stone at the touch of the sun, and even if her skin did burn, she wouldn't be on this mortal coil long enough for it to become cancerous.

Still. The light did make the darkness easier, whatever reason they'd gifted it to her, and if she didn't mind a lungful of pain and agony, she could even draw enough power from the daylight to make navy blue and royal purple and winter teal lights sparkle over the iron manacle around her right wrist.

If she didn't mind the lungful of

pain, she could even make the lights bright enough to camouflage the red welts the manacle was causing, raised and raw in places and burning like a thousand fiery suns when she let her concentration slip and couldn't block it out.

Of course, if she simply decided not to eat, her wrist would heal up and it would be just fine. But the bastards kept leaving her food just inside the heavy wooden door, right at the full stretch of her reach, and she had to lean her full weight against the chain that bound her to the window's wall to even have a hope of hooking her foot around the wedge of dry bread, or snagging the occasional lump of burnt offal that she supposed counted as her protein intake.

She'd always imagined food to be much more pleasurable, somehow, to taste of something better than dry dust and charred ash.

Fie, that mortal worlds demanded mortal rites. Life was so much simpler when your body took care of its own needs, imbibing pure energy from pure surrounds.

Of course, that was the problem, she added, sniffing disdainfully as the acrid scent of plastic smoke from a garbage fire in the neighbour's yard wound its way into the room.

The mortal coil was hardly 'pure surroundings' by any stretch of the imagination. And that meant that one had to shut oneself off to said surroundings, requisiting physical consumption of energy in the form of food, and severely hampering one's ability to draw on environmental energy to perform what mortals laughably called 'magic'.

Frustrating, and after thirty-six days, nearly enough to make one wish to resign.

Outside, beyond the house's yard,

probably on the path that bordered the pond, someone with light steps and shoes too large for their feet clip-clopped around the edge of the pond, trit-trot-trit-trot-trit.

Ava stiffened.

The darkness strained, reaching for the child… but Ava batted it away with her lights, inhaling sharply against the pain that she could only block out so long as she didn't hold onto said lights for too long.

The footsteps passed on, and Ava allowed her spine to relax again, exhaling even as the darkness coiled about her again.

Another child, safe.

Jaw twitching, Ava let her head tilt back against the plasterboard under the window. Her nostrils flared as the pain tried to creep through her awareness. She shoved it aside, and went back to waiting.

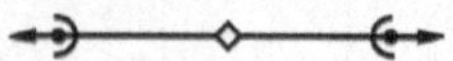

It was funny, the way her captors thought they had the better deal. Ava thought they had the better deal too, but that was because she knew what was coming—and her goals differed dramatically from theirs.

Thirty-six days ago now, Ava had arrived at this pitiful excuse of a house, with its sagging corrugated-iron porch and spiralling, destructive ivy and worn-down weatherboard walls, at the end of a little dirt laneway in a quiet, innocuous town where nothing much happened of note except by way of the usual mortal strifes and laments, and, idly brushing cobwebs from her shoulders as the last of the immortal realms fell away around her, Ava had stepped through the peeling picket gate under the arbour of tangled greenery at the front of the little house.

Stupid, they were, to have left the

sign there on the arbour proclaiming welcome to any who wished to enter, allowing her to circumvent their hearth protection entirely—but she supposed that, to fulfil their nefarious intents, they had to let their barriers down to some degree.

And who knew? Perhaps these were some of the many mortals who lived their lives blithely unaware of their own magic, of the way their hearths gathered energy around them, of the way their homes reflected their inner state of being and the role of hearth magic in protecting them from harm.

Of course, this was not a house designed to protect *anyone* from harm, and that was precisely why Ava was here.

This was the kind of house whose insides *perfectly* reflected its occupants—and that was the problem.

For there were some harms—murder, for instance—that rippled outwards from the mortal realm, the energies dispelled sloshing over into the immortal worlds and affecting the balances there as well.

There were acts of goodness, too, that did the same, and beyond that, supreme acts of love and self-sacrifice that changed all worlds for the better.

But then there were dark things, deeds made possible only by taking the goodness and purity of an innocent and twisting it against them—genuine acts of evil.

Such things not only sent ripples through the realms, they sent a smoke-cloud, a stain permeating through all layers of reality—and immortal beings gathered there like flies.

Some gathered there to feed, to taste the salty, smoky blackness and rejoice—the ones who'd chosen already to serve their own darknesses forever.

Others came as spectators, immortal lives drawn to mortal conflict like the humans to their bloodsports.

Still more came for research, a bid to gather data to inform their own long-played decisions.

Sometimes these ones fretted, concerned by what they saw; every so often, one of them would break, would throw themselves into the cloud in an attempt to interfere…

But that never ended well. These things could be influenced, of course, but one needed proper training before carelessly flinging oneself at the mortal coil.

Finally, then, were the others, the ones who had already chosen the light, the ones who had perhaps always been faithful, or who had strayed but returned like a lost child eager to be comforted by a loving parent. They came to the black places too, and in the dim silver light of the immortal plane, they took their vows as the consummation of their training, and they crossed through the darkness into the burning, polluted, choking air of the mortal world, clothed in bodies that could not die, but which still could hurt, and hunger, and tire.

Such was Ava, as she was sometimes called, and as she sat in the empty room on threadbare carpet in the golden glow of the early evening light and found the sound of her heartbeat, she knew that an end drew nigh.

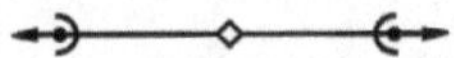

The door opened, silent on heavy hinges.

Ava supposed that silent hinges took away any possibility of warning the usual occupants of the room, the ones who rolled and tossed in the too-small bed away in the far corner, too far for her to reach it with her chain.

If the intruder's feet were silent enough, it might be that the first warning the too-small, too-young occupants had was a hand, heavy on their shoulder, or perhaps gripping their upper arm.

Ava could still taste the lingering traces of their terror, feeding strength to the darkness around her—darkness that she had slowly, bit by bit, been reading, like a very dense and very awful book, packing away what she learned into the secrecy of her deep purple lights for later use.

This time, though, instead of an anonymous arm delivering a hunk of desiccated bread and noxious-tasting water, a man entered—*the* man, or at least one of them, innocuous looking as befitted his crimes, of average height and slightly heavier than average build, with a weak chin and close-set eyes that gleamed hawkishly in the evening light.

He closed the door behind him and looked down at Ava with something approaching delighted anticipation, if something so perverse could ever be twinned with delight. "Hello, lovely," he said, and the rich suggestion in his voice set the intangible darkness practically thrumming. "I've come to have some fun with you."

Ava sniffed. "No."

"I don't think you understand," he said. "You're trapped. Chained to the wall. There's nothing you can do to stop me."

Ava smiled, her teeth gleaming in the darkness. "Oh yes," she said silkily. "You have me. And how many children have you managed to lure to this place since I arrived? Tell me that?"

The man opened his mouth, but stopped to frown. "Irrelevant," he said.

"Since you arrived, we haven't been trying. Decided it was safer, with you here. Less likely to get caught."

Ava licked the corner of her mouth delicately. "First," she said, "if you wish to think that you made that choice, so be it. And second..." She stood, the chain clanking and rattling like the uncoiling of doom. "*You* are not here to have fun with *me*. *I* am here to have fun with *you*."

Not that it was supposed to be fun. That was a little wrong of her, to insinuate that. But he'd left the line wide open for her, and mortals did so appreciate such irony—and so, she knew, did the immortals who would be watching this place keenly from above. Her boss was the forgiving sort, even if he might be somewhat disappointed.

The man laughed, a piercing, filthy thing, and Ava could practically feel it crawling up her spine.

She spat, removing the taste of charred promises from her mouth. "Will you turn from your ways and beg for forgiveness?" she said. "Even now, that way is open to you."

Her stomach roiled, bile rising in her throat, but she had to make the offer. And occasionally, they took it, these people consumed by their darknesses—and she had seen that when they did, they made the more fearsome warriors of all for the cause of the light.

So she made the offer—but when he laughed again and spat right back—at her, though, not at the floor as she had done—she was hardly surprised.

"Very well, then," she said, and closed her eyes.

She took a deep breath—and fear coursed through her like ice.

This was going to hurt.

Ava shoved the fear aside, and let down her barriers.

The energy of the world around her rushed in, some filthy, some stained, some polluted—but so, so much of it still clean, and pure, and beautiful. It filled her, beaming through her like sunlight into crystal, and she inhaled deeply.

It hurt, burning like nothing she'd ever felt in the immortal realm, but this, *this* was what she'd trained for, and her master had given her the authority for vengeance, and she was going to take it.

The man screamed as teal and navy lightning hit him in the chest.

Ava smiled, eyes narrowing as she watching the lights that had streaked from her outstretched hand play over him for a moment longer before dying away. "You like that?" she said—then remembered that she was not supposed to gloat.

She exhaled loudly through her nostrils.

Another bolt of lightning hit the man, arcing from her hand to his face.

It hurt, the pain searing through her head like someone driving a nail in—but it hurt him more.

He collapsed to the floor.

Before Ava could take a step, his compatriot rushed in. This man, taller, greyer, drier and more worn, glanced briefly at his fellow on the floor, then stared up at Ava. He licked his lips. "Um," he said.

Ava gave him a tight smile too and —refraining from gloating entirely, even though her chest was practically going to burn up with satisfaction at this point—she sent a bolt of lightning toward him also.

He fell instantly, right to the ground next to the first man—and now, Ava stepped closer.

Closer, closer, all the way across the room until she stood over the men, frozen in place on the floor but still alive, still conscious—still perfectly capable of staring up at her in horror, eyes saucered, unable to move anything else.

Ava narrowed her eyes. "You know what the best part is?" she said softly —not gloating, just offering them the facts. "That wasn't even the most painful bit. This is."

Swiftly, she bent, and royal purple light trickled from her fingers.

It wreathed the two men, circling them as though seeking something in particular—which it seemed to find right in their temples.

The light sank into their heads, vanishing from view.

But their eyes stretched open even wider—and now their mouths did too, stretching in silent screams.

Ava waited. It would be a long wait, because there had been a long, long list of victims—and although she wasn't allowed to gloat, she *was* allowed to do this: to let them feel the pain—condensed, by necessity—of every single child they'd molested in this place.

They began to writhe on the floor, horror-ridden caterpillars, ugly, pale worms—for a few minutes longer, anyway.

Then the purple light began to break through, fine cracks appearing in their skin all over, widening, widening as the light pulsed outward.

There was a sudden pop. The air pressure in the room intensified.

Ava tasted metal at the back of her throat, at the tip of her tongue.

And then the pressure vanished— and so did the men, exploding silently into dust motes of purple and teal and navy light that drifted gently down toward the floor.

Most times, Ava and her kin could do nothing.

Most times, they, like everyone else, were consigned to simply watch as evil had its way with the world. The course must be run, the master said. The consequences must be acknowledged.

But sometimes—just sometimes—she was allowed to watch that evil burn.

And honestly?

It was far, far more satisfying than Hell.

THE MAKING OF *FAR MORE SATISFYING THAN HELL*

This story shares a similarity with Inklet #8, *A Final Request For Mercy*, in that they are both me seeking to make sense of, or at least respond in some way to, real-world events.

That other story came after the family dog got into the family rabbit hutch.

This story came after a conversation with someone about things they had experienced as a child—things that no child should ever have to experience.

I couldn't do anything to change this person's past. I couldn't even really do much to change their present, except provide a supportive listening ear. And it wouldn't be helpful of me to share my frustration, my feelings of anger and helplessness, with them too much: they didn't need the burden of helping me second-hand process their trauma while they were still very much in the throes of trying to process it themselves.

So I did what I, as a writer, could do: I wrote this story, as a way of processing things for myself, as a fantasy of a world where justice might be served, as an expression of hope for and belief in all those people out there fighting to protect the innocent of our world.

It still frustrates me that justice is not mine to mete out. But if absolutely nothing else, there is solace, still, in fiction—and catharsis.

Read more by Amy Laurens!

CRYSTALLINE AND BRIGHT

I stood, staring down into the teal-blue river water, ignoring the chatter behind my back. The snow covered the ground around me, hiding bumps and ridges, soothing out sharp edges. To my right, the dark stone shadow of the bridge stood like a guardian, watchful, alert. Snow rimmed its edges; every so often some shifted in a sudden breeze and landed in the quiet river below with a gentle splash.

The willows on the far bank slept quietly under their snow blanket, their green sappy smell hidden by the cold, sharp scent of the snow.

Stop.

Start again.

It wasn't actually winter. It was early spring, with the grass green and new, the sound of a lawnmower buzzing in the distance and the scent of cut grass drifting on the wind. Moss covered the shadowed side of the old stone bridge, and willows stretched their fingers to the slow-moving, drowsy little river that bordered the grounds of the school.

A butterfly flittered past, white wings speckled with black like soot.

The world felt fresh, and green, and full of promise.

I was still ignoring the chattering behind me.

Stop.

Start again.

It's summer, and the air is swelteringly hot. Sweat drips down the back of my neck, pools under my arms, under my awkward breasts. The river in front of me is milky-blue, gentle, quiet, and I long to strip off my shirt and jeans and throw myself into the water.

It's not just the breathtakingly sharp cold of the icemelt I'm craving; it's the feeling of being *clean*.

The air stinks of a fish that Lander left out on the bank near the bridge, rotting to pieces in the high temperatures.

I'm still ignoring the chatter.

Stop.

Let's try once more.

It's autumn—of course—and the willows have turned yellow, their little leaves dropping into the milk-water, eddying slowly away from the shadow of the bridge.

Behind me, the emerald lawn of the old school buildings is ringed with gem-toned maples, butter-leafed poplars, silver-and-gold birches. Occasionally, the wind catches stray leaves and flings them into the pond.

I can still hear the voices behind me.

All of these pictures are true, and none of them are.

Not precisely, not uniquely; they're all composites, the merging and piecing together of hundreds of memories of similar experiences, of all the times I stood on the river bank and stared longingly into its depths, imagining myself a naiad with a secret home to return to, somewhere people loved me.

These images have to be composites, because for every time I was down at the river, I was focusing only on two things: ignoring the voices, and watching the water.

All the other details, the little bits of specificity that allow me to recall the place in so much explicit detail? I never noticed them at the time.

And so I have to piece them together, collage-fashion, or else I have nothing to say. Nothing to see.

Nothing except the water, milky-blue that occasionally, in the right light, at the right time of day, flashed teal and came alive.

I'd lived with the voices as long as I could remember. Some of them were real, inasmuch as they belonged to real, live people whom other people could see, who grew and developed and changed with the passing of the seasons; some of them were *sur*real, inasmuch as they belonged to people I could see, but that none other could, and who did not change or grow with the passing of the seasons.

And some of the voices… Some of them I could never divine exactly what they were.

But all of them, real, surreal and unknown, had one thing in common: none of them liked me.

I could never figure out why. Oh, sure, I came to the school without the name and pedigree of any of the other students, a supposed-orphan with no memory of her life before double digits and no connections to speak of. I wasn't part of their circle, my excellent trust fund notwithstanding, and so the real people, the live people, couldn't accept me.

It shouldn't have been that way. It seemed to me that I hadn't done anything wrong, or untoward, hadn't neglected to do anything needed, hadn't slighted or snubbed any who hadn't already done so several times to me.

And yet, for all the years I was there at the school, its grand, lofty double-storey buildings made from pale stone like a castle, ivy creeping all about like Christmas lights, the lawn constantly emerald, the hedges consistently clipped… For all those composite years, no one ever liked me.

Well, a slight exaggeration: my teachers liked me well enough. I was a diligent student.

And the river liked me. I could tell that, because when I was close to the river, the other voices kept their distance—and the river had a voice of its own. And once or twice, I could have sworn it also had a face.

Keep reading! Head to www.inkprintpress.com/ amylaurens/aprilshowers/ to buy your copy now!

ABOUT THE AUTHOR

AMY LAURENS is an Australian author of fantasy fiction for all ages. Her novella *Bones Of The Sea* was shortlisted for the 2021 Aurealis Awards.

In addition, Amy has written the award-winning portal-fantasy *Sanctuary* series about Edge, a 13-year-old girl forced to move to a small country town because of witness protection (the first book is *Where Shadows Rise*), the humorous fantasy *Kaditeos* series, following newly graduated Evil Overlord Mercury as she attempts to acquire a castle, the young adult series *Storm Foxes*, about love and magic and family in small town Australia, and a whole host of non-fiction.

INKLETS

Collect them all! Released on the 1st and 15th of each month.

Shadows NEVER LIE
AMY LAURENS

Here She Lies
LIANA BROOKS

Perfect Destruction
An Age Of Unicorns Story
AMY LAURENS

What Blood Can Do
AMY LAURENS

Dancer, Dreamer Seer
LIANA BROOKS

As Time Whirls Slowly Past
AMY LAURENS

Far More Satisfying Than Hell
AMY LAURENS

Just Another Day In Hell
LIANA BROOKS

Moon AND Morning
AMY LAURENS

INKLET #088
Some
Impropriety
Expected
AMY LAURENS

INKLET #089
NEON SNOW
LIANA BROOKS

INKLET #090
Reincarnation
LIANA BROOKS

INKLET #091
More Than
Mushrooms
AMY LAURENS

DOUBLE ISSUE
INKLET #092
How To Make A Star
& The World Ended
LIANA BROOKS

INKLET #093
CAUGHT
IN THE ACT
AMY LAURENS

INKLET #094
ANUBIS
Has Sent You
Six Souls
LIANA BROOKS

INKLET #095
PRAYER TO A
GODDESS
LIANA BROOKS

INKLET #096
Love In The
Time Of Corona
AMY LAURENS